Copyright © 2020 Lindsay Ann Fink.

All rights reserved. No part of this book may be used or reproduced by any means, graphic, electronic, or mechanical, including photocopying, recording, taping or by any information storage retrieval system without the written permission of the author except in the case of brief quotations embodied in critical articles and reviews.

Balboa Press books may be ordered through booksellers or by contacting:

Balboa Press
A Division of Hay House
1663 Liberty Drive
Bloomington, IN 47403
www.balboapress.com
1 (877) 407-4847

Because of the dynamic nature of the Internet, any web addresses or links contained in this book may have changed since publication and may no longer be valid. The views expressed in this work are solely those of the author and do not necessarily reflect the views of the publisher, and the publisher hereby disclaims any responsibility for them.

Any people depicted in stock imagery provided by Getty Images are models, and such images are being used for illustrative purposes only. Certain stock imagery © Getty Images.

ISBN: 978-1-9822-5131-4 (sc)
ISBN: 978-1-9822-5132-1 (e)

Library of Congress Control Number: 2020913314

Print information available on the last page.

Balboa Press rev. date: 08/19/2020

BALBOA.PRESS

Thomas the Turkey

Lindsay Ann Fink

Thomas the turkey had woken up early on Thanksgiving morning. His whole family was coming to have dinner together. But right before his guests were due to arrive, Thomas realizes that his feathers are lost! Can you help him retrace his steps and find the missing feathers?

This morning, Thomas woke
up and brushed his beak.

Then Thomas made some
cereal for breakfast.

After breakfast, he took
out the trash. He is such
a helpful turkey!

Then Thomas played
with some toys.

It still wasn't time for Thomas's annual tradition of watching the Thanksgiving Day Parade, so he decided to read a book.

By the time he had finished reading, it was time for the parade! Thomas sat on the couch in the living room.

The parade was so exciting that it made Thomas sleepy. He lay down to take a nap. Night-night, Thomas.

When Thomas woke from his nap, the dinner table was all set for Thanksgiving dinner. Can you guess what was in the center of the table? The rest of his feathers! Yay!

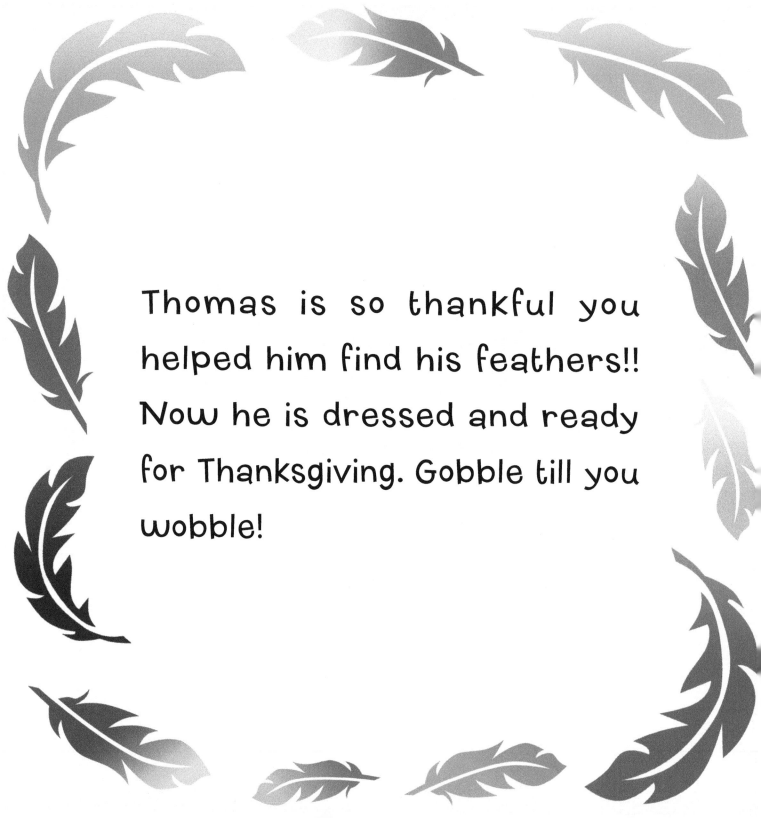

Thomas is so thankful you helped him find his feathers!! Now he is dressed and ready for Thanksgiving. Gobble till you wobble!

This book is a fun interactive feather hunt. Before you read the book with your little one, make sure to hide a feather in the bathroom sink, a feather near the breakfast cereal, a feather near the trash bin, a feather near some toys, a feather near some books, a feather on the couch, and a feather on your child's bed. (This should all be set up before you read the book.) Depending on the age of your children, try to make it easy or hard to find the feathers, or you can ask the older children to be in charge of setting up the missing feathers before the story begins. Happy feather hunting and happy Thanksgiving! We are thankful to you, our readers, for taking part in this fun feather hunt.

Thank you Meghan McLaughlin Scott for designing these
beautiful feathers. They are as colorful as you are!

I am Thankful for my three little Turkeys for inspiring me to create this fun-filled feather hunt.

I am truly grateful for super G and Pop Pop for always being so generous and supportive of my dreams.

To my readers, I am thankful you have chosen this story to read - it means the world to me.

Please tell me, what are you thankful for?

CPSIA information can be obtained
at www.ICGtesting.com
Printed in the USA
BVHW021733210920
589277BV00002B/3

9 781982 251314